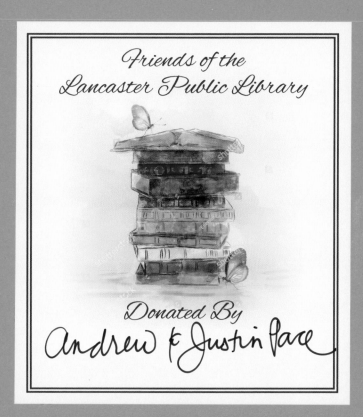

My
Tree

Hope Lim

Pictures by
Il Sung Na

NEAL PORTER BOOKS
HOLIDAY HOUSE / NEW YORK

For Raphael and Sophia —H.L.

For Lulu —I.S.N.

Neal Porter Books

Text copyright © 2021 by Hope Lim
Illustrations copyright © 2021 by Il Sung Na
All Rights Reserved
HOLIDAY HOUSE is registered in the U.S. Patent and Trademark Office.
Printed and bound in January 2021 at C & C Offset, Shenzhen, China.
The artwork for this book was made using digital media.
Book design by Jennifer Browne
www.holidayhouse.com
First Edition
1   3   5   7   9   10   8   6   4   2

Library of Congress Cataloging-in-Publication Data

Names: Lim, Hope, author. | Na, Il Sung, illustrator.
Title: My tree / by Hope Lim ; illustrated by Il Sung Na.
Description: First edition. | New York : Holiday House, [2021] | "A Neal
Porter Book." | Audience: Ages 4 to 8. | Audience: Grades K–1. |
Summary: "A boy makes a connection with a plum tree after moving to a
new home"— Provided by publisher.
Identifiers: LCCN 2020025776 | ISBN 9780823443383 (hardcover)
Subjects: CYAC: Plum—Fiction. | Trees—Fiction. | Korean
Americans—Fiction.
Classification: LCC PZ7.1.L5524 My 2021 | DDC [E]—dc23
LC record available at https://lccn.loc.gov/2020025776

ISBN 978-0-8234-4338-3 (hardcover)

In the backyard of our new home stood an old tree.
Tall, crooked, quiet.
It reminded me of the persimmon tree
that shaded our porch in Korea.
Deep purple plums dotted every branch.
So I named her Plumee.

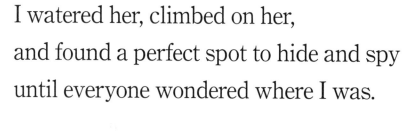

I watered her, climbed on her,
and found a perfect spot to hide and spy
until everyone wondered where I was.

I spent my first day in America with Plumee.

And she became my tree.

Whenever I missed my home in Korea,

Plumee lifted me up,

and I played on her branches.

In the summer, I watched the sk
through her thick green leaves.

In the spring, I celebrated
my birthday under her
blooming white flowers.

In the fall, I picked purple plums and shared them with neighbors.

In the winter, I listened to the wind whistling through her dark brown branches.

Plumee made me feel at home.

One spring night, a rainstorm with high winds
swept through the city and knocked down
many trees, old and new.

Plumee fell down that night.

The next morning, I saw Plumee lying in the middle
of the yard, away from the house, away from the deck,
and away from the fence.
Her roots were pulled out of the earth, worn out and sad.
"An old tree knows how to lie down when it's time,"
my Grandma had told me in Korea.

I climbed on Plumee and stood on her.
How immense she looked under my feet!

For days, she turned into everything I wished for.
A tree house.
A rocket.

An island.

A ship.
Neighborhood kids joined in,
and we all had fun . . .

. . . until a little boy scraped his arm and cried.
And then it was time for Plumee to go.

The next day, Plumee was hauled away.
Without Plumee, everything felt different.

No more white flowers, no more green shade,
no more purple plums or whistling wind,
and no more secret hiding place.

In the middle of the yard
I stood alone,
remembering Plumee,
tall,
crooked,
quiet.

"Daddy, I miss Plumee."
Daddy nodded and squeezed my hand.
A few days later, we planted a new plum tree,
short and straight, in Plumee's old place.

I watered her and patted down the soil.
I wondered if she would ever know an old tree
once stood where her roots were spreading.
I watered her more, and she grew little by little.

Then one spring day, I saw something familiar.
The new plum tree had her first blossoms.
Fresh white flowers dotted every branch
and fluttered in the breeze.
The new tree was short and straight,
but donned in milky petals,
she stood quiet,
like Plumee.

"Hello," I whispered.

In the backyard of our home stands a young plum tree.
I water her and watch her grow tall and strong.
And I feel right at home.